Up to the skies

and down again

For Lily - with love
N.M.

For my father
David

Uᴘ ᴛᴏ ᴛʜᴇ sᴋɪᴇs ᴀɴᴅ ᴅᴏᴡɴ ᴀɢᴀɪɴ
Written by Nanette Newman
Illustrated by Sam Williams
British Library Cataloguing in Publication Data
A catalogue record of this book is available from the British Library
ISBN 0 340 72269 X (HB)
ISBN 0 340 72654 7 (PB)
Text copyright © Nanette Newman 1999
Illustrations copyright © Sam Williams 1999

First edition published 1999
10 9 8 7 6 5 4 3 2 1

Published by Hodder Children's Books,
a division of Hodder Headline plc,
338 Euston Road, London NW1 3BH
Printed in Hong Kong

Up to the skies

and down again

Nanette Newman

Illustrated by Sam Williams

Hodder
Children's
Books

A division of Hodder Headline plc

When I was born and
came out of your tummy,

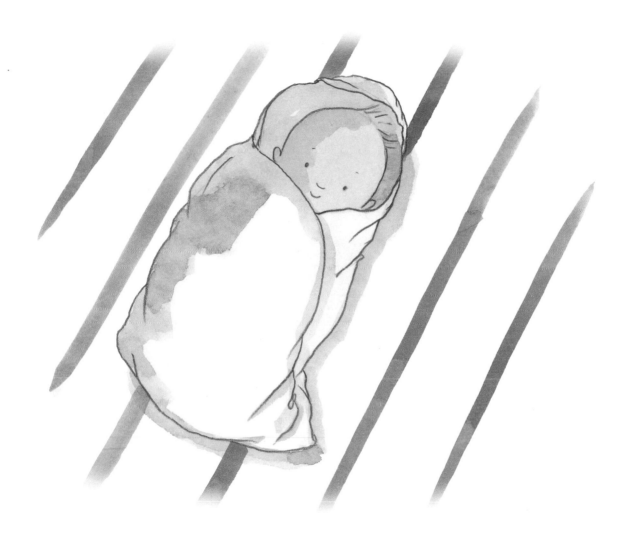

Did you say, 'I'm so happy,
and glad I'm your mummy?'

Did some of your friends say,
'Oh, isn't she sweet!

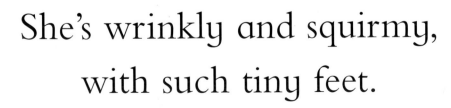

She's wrinkly and squirmy,
with such tiny feet.

When will her hair grow?
Are her eyes brown or blue?

Oh, look, is she smiling
at me, or at you?'

Did my daddy say,
'Yes, that's a really nice baby.
Will she sleep through the night?'
(And did you say, 'Maybe'?)

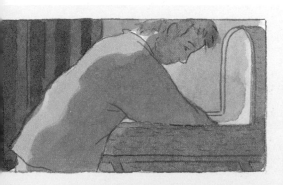

And when I was cross,
or grizzly, or screamy. . .

Did they say, 'Does she look like

her mum or dad?'

As the months went on by,
did I try to be funny?

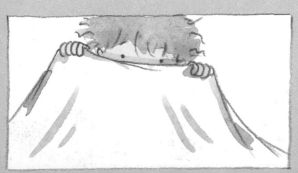

Did I wriggle my toes?
Did you tickle my tummy?